Rain Forests

Philip Sauvain

 Carolrhoda Books, Inc. / Minneapolis

All words that appear in **bold** are explained in the glossary that starts on page 30.

Photographs courtesy of: Forest Management Foundation 27t; Forest Stewardship Council 25t; Friends of the Earth / Nick Cobbing 24; The Hutchison Library / Jeremy A.Horner 10br; / Richard House 21c; Impact Photos / Christophe Bluntzer 9t; / Colin Jones 9b; / Alain Everard 10bl; / A.Lorgnier/Visa 12bl, 13t; / Michael Mirecki 14b; / Mark Henley 19; / S.Gutierrez/Cedri 20b; / Robert Gibbs 26t; Philip A.Sauvain 5bl & r; South American Pictures / Tony Morrison 14t, 18t, 25b, 28t; Still Pictures / Mark Edwards - cover, 26b, 28b; / Edward Parker - title page, 7t, 18b; / T de Salis 5t; / Daniel Dancer 7b; / Carstea Rabbek 10bc; / Michel Gunther 11tl, 16b; / Louise Murray 11tr; / Alan Watson 11b; / Alain Compost 12t & br; / Regis Cavignaux 13b; / Nigel Dickinson 15t; / Margaret Wilson 15b; / Paul Harrison 16t, 17; / Dario Novellino 20t; / John Maier 21t, 27b.

Illustrations and maps by David Hogg.

This edition first published in the United States in 1996 by Carolrhoda Books, Inc.

A ZOË BOOK

Copyright © 1996 Zoë Books Limited. Originally produced in 1996 by Zoë Books Limited, Winchester, England.

Carolrhoda Books, Inc., c/o The Lerner Group
241 First Avenue North, Minneapolis, MN 55401

Library of Congress Cataloging-in-Publication Data

Sauvain, Philip Arthur.
    [Rainforest]
    Rain forests / by Philip Sauvain.
        p. cm. — (Geography detective)
    Previously published as: Rainforest. 1996.
    "A Zoë book" — T.p. verso.
    Includes index.
    Summary: Describes the world's rain forests, including the plants, animals, and people found there, with case studies of specific forests.
    ISBN 1-57505-041-2 (lib. bdg. : alk. paper)
        1. Rain forest ecology — Juvenile literature. 2. Rain forests — Juvenile literature. [1. Rain forests. 2. Rain forest ecology. 3. Ecology.]
I. Title. II. Series.
QH541.5.R27S27 1997
574.5'2642 — dc20   96-10915

Printed in Italy by Grafedit SpA.
Bound in the United States of America
1 2 3 4 5 6 02 01 00 99 98 97

Contents

What Is a Rain Forest?

Imagine you are standing in a thick, green forest full of the sounds of strange birds and animals. It is hot and damp, and the light is dim beneath the huge trees. When you look around, you see hundreds of different plants growing on and among the trees. This is what it is like in a **tropical rain forest**.

Rain forests have five layers. The thickest layer is the **canopy**. This is where the crowns, or tops, of the tallest trees meet and form a roof above the forest. Very little sunlight reaches the layers below the canopy.

● Researchers found 1,500 different kinds of plants, 150 kinds of butterflies, 400 kinds of birds, 125 kinds of mammals, and 100 kinds of reptiles in only 600 acres of South American rain forest.

▼ This illustration shows the five layers of a tropical rain forest.

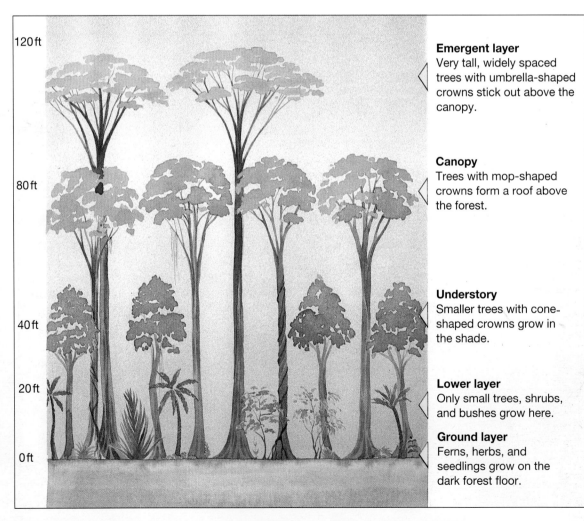

120 ft

Emergent layer
Very tall, widely spaced trees with umbrella-shaped crowns stick out above the canopy.

80 ft

Canopy
Trees with mop-shaped crowns form a roof above the forest.

40 ft

Understory
Smaller trees with cone-shaped crowns grow in the shade.

20 ft

Lower layer
Only small trees, shrubs, and bushes grow here.

0 ft

Ground layer
Ferns, herbs, and seedlings grow on the dark forest floor.

● Not all rain forests are in tropical regions. Some grow in cooler areas of the world such as the Pacific Coast of Washington. In these **temperate rain forests**, many of the trees have needle-shaped leaves and are coniferous, or cone-bearing. Like the broad-leaved trees in tropical rain forests, most trees in temperate rain forests are evergreens.

Each layer of the forest is the habitat, or home, of different plants and animals. Together, these habitats make up the whole forest **environment**. All parts of the environment — the plants, animals, soil, and climate — are linked together to form the rain-forest **ecosystem**. If one part of the ecosystem changes, all the other parts are likely to be affected too.

Geography Detective

Which of the three photographs on this page was taken in a tropical rain forest? Which one shows coniferous trees? Two of the photographs show evergreen trees, which have leaves all year round. The third picture shows trees that shed their leaves every year. These are called deciduous trees. In woods or forests near your home, are most of the trees evergreen or deciduous? In what season of the year do deciduous trees lose their leaves?

Where Are Rain Forests?

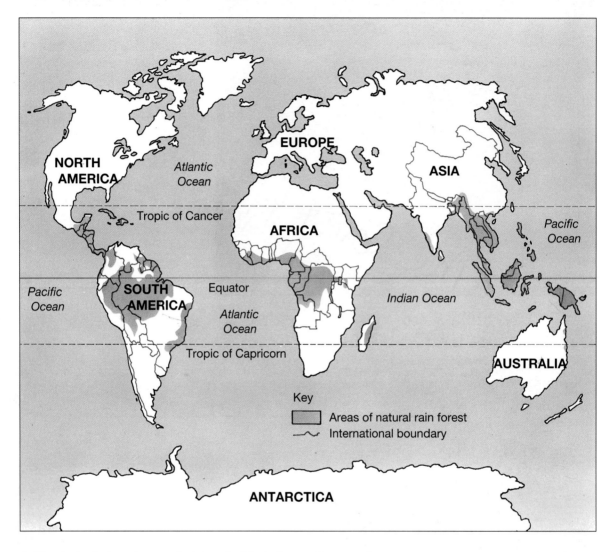

▲ Tropical rain forests grow in areas that lie between the **equator** and the **tropics**.

The map above shows the parts of the world where tropical rain forests grow naturally. The climate in these places is hot and wet all year. The largest rain forest in the world is in the valley of the Amazon River in South America. The forest covers more than one million square miles. This area is about a third of the size of either the United States or Canada and is about half the size of Australia.

● Tropical rain forests cover about 6 percent of the earth's land surface.

◀ The Ndian River flows through the rain forest in Cameroon, a country in West Africa.

◀ This temperate rain forest is in Washington. Temperate rain forests grow in cool regions that lie farther north or south of the equator than tropical rain forests.

Geography Detective

The red lines on the map on page 6 show the boundaries of all the rain-forest countries. Use an atlas or a globe to find their names. Name two rain-forest countries in South America, Africa, and Asia. Name one other continent where tropical rain forests grow.

Rain-forest Climate

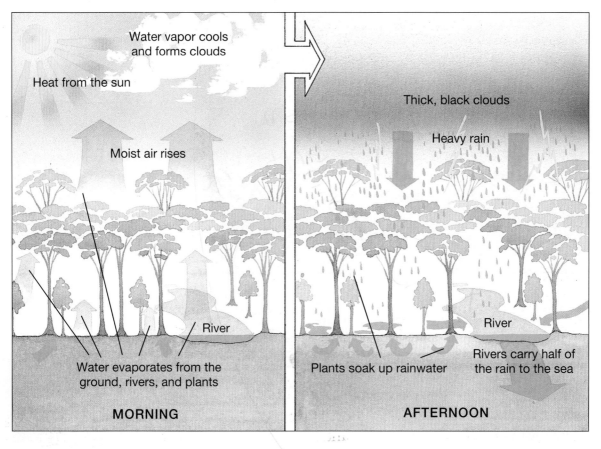

Water vapor cools and forms clouds

Heat from the sun

Moist air rises

River

Water evaporates from the ground, rivers, and plants

MORNING

Thick, black clouds

Heavy rain

River

Plants soak up rainwater

Rivers carry half of the rain to the sea

AFTERNOON

Tropical rain forests grow in hot places where at least 80 inches of rain fall every year. The average monthly temperature in these areas is 78° F. With no seasons such as summer and winter, the weather stays much the same all year round.

Each day in a rain forest begins hot and cloudless. By noon it is even hotter. Water **evaporates** in the heat and turns into water vapor. As the vapor rises, it cools and forms tiny droplets of water in the form of clouds. By the afternoon, the clouds are thick and black. Thunder crashes overhead, and torrents of rain fall. The rain usually stops in the evening, and the air is cooler. This weather pattern is repeated day after day.

▲ This illustration shows the daily weather pattern in a tropical rain forest.

● Scientists at weather stations all over the world measure temperature and rainfall every day. Some weather stations in tropical forests have recorded over 300 inches of rain in one year. This is enough to fill a bucket 26 feet high!

● Temperatures in tropical rain forests are high all year round. During the day, they may rise higher than 85° F. At night they rarely drop below 68° F.

A woman walks through heavy rain in Bali, Indonesia. She carries a load of produce on her head.

About half the rain that falls in rain forests eventually flows into the nearest sea through rivers. The rest is used by trees and plants.

▼ Rain-forest waterways often flood. That is why buildings near the rivers are usually built on stilts.

Geography Detective

You can learn more about evaporation at home. Put a small amount of water into a saucer. Place it in a warm room or outside when the weather is warm. Use a clock or watch to figure out how long it takes for the water to evaporate. Then do the same thing again, but put the saucer in a cool place. How much longer does it take for the water to evaporate when the air is cool?

Rain-forest Plants

Thousands of different species, or types, of plants and animals live in tropical rain forests. This variety of life is called **biodiversity**. Most species are well adapted, or suited, to the environment they live in. In rain forests, for example, many trees and plants have glossy, waxy leaves with pointed ends called drip tips. These features help water run off leaves quickly.

Two main groups of plants are adapted to living in rain forests. Both groups use trees for support and as a way to reach the sunny canopy. One group includes creepers and climbers whose roots grow in the ground. These plants are called **lianas**. The other group includes plants such as orchids, ferns, and mosses. Called **epiphytes**, these plants grow on the surface of trees and other plants and

● Rain forests contain more than half the world's species of plants.

● Many rain-forest plants contain substances that can be used as medicines. Forest-dwelling peoples use them all the time. Some plants, such as the cinchona tree, are grown on plantations (large farms) in Southeast Asia. The quinine that comes from the bark of the cinchona tree is collected and used to treat malaria and other diseases.

▲ Tropical orchids thrive in Southeast Asia.

▶ The Toucan's Bill flower grows in Bolivia, South America.

All the plants shown here grow in tropical rain forests.

◀ This flower grows in the rain forest in Ecuador, South America.

10

▲ Many different types of epiphytes grow on tree branches in rain forests. The plants use the branches for support.

▲ Lianas wind around tree trunks and branches to reach the sunlight in the canopy.

get water and food from the air and from rain. Some epiphytes have sword-shaped leaves that grow in tight clusters to trap water. These epiphytes are called **bromeliads**.

▼ Tree roots called buttress roots often grow 15 feet above the ground and spread out the same distance on the ground. The roots help to support the tall trunks of rain-forest trees.

Geography Detective

Are there places in your community where tropical plants grow? You might see some in a botanical garden, a zoo, a shopping mall, a garden center, or even at home. Visit some of these places and draw some of the tropical plants you find. Label your drawings to show how the plants have adapted to hot, damp conditions.

Rain-forest Animals

Most rain-forest birds and mammals live high in the canopy. More light and more food are available in the treetops than in the lower layers of the forest.

Many different creatures live in the understory. Some of these animals, such as chimpanzees, are large. Others, such as wild cats, ocelots, snakes, and tree frogs, are smaller. They all live mostly above the ground and use lianas to move through the trees. The largest creatures, such as forest elephants and tigers, live on the ground.

Rain-forest animals are well adapted to living in the trees. They use their claws, hooked paws, or long tails to grip the branches. The vine snake, for example, travels from one tree to another by stiffening its body into a long rod to cross the gap.

▲ Flying squirrels open a cloak of skin to fly from tree to tree in the rain forest. The tail helps the animal to steer, like a rudder on a boat.

▲ A lemur grips onto a tree in Madagascar, an island off the southeastern coast of Africa.

▲ This orangutan swings with its baby from one branch to another in the Indonesian rain forest.

▶ Creatures such as the chameleon look so much like the undergrowth in which they live that it is hard for other animals to see them. This camouflage, or disguise, helps to keep prey safe from the animals who hunt them.

● Rain-forest areas that are rich in biodiversity are sometimes called hot spots. Scientists believe that the rain forests of the Amazon region in South America, for example, have over one million species of plants and animals.

● Some rain-forest animals live in only one part of the world. For example, the toucan (a bird) lives only in South America, and the aye-aye (a lemur) lives only in Madagascar.

Case Study

The orangutan is an ape that lives on the islands of Borneo and Sumatra in Southeast Asia. In the Malay language, the ape's name means "man of the forest." The orangutan has long, narrow hands and feet. It uses its long arms to swing through the trees in search of food. It eats fruits and leaves. At night it makes a nest of leaves in the treetops to sleep in.

The orangutan is an **endangered species** because its forest habitat is being destroyed. About 20,000 orangutans live in protected forest **wildlife reserves**.

Geography Detective

The hummingbird in this picture lives in the rain forests of South America. In what ways is the bird adapted to feed on nectar from flowers? Look up information about tarsiers (a small rain-forest mammal) in an encyclopedia. Make a list of how tarsiers are adapted to living in rain forests.

Peoples of the Rain Forests

The first peoples to live in the tropical rain forests, thousands of years ago, were **hunter-gatherers**. The descendants of these peoples still live in the world's rain forests. Each group has its own name and customs.

These forest peoples know which plants and animals to eat and how to hunt and gather for food. They also know which plants to use to make medicines. Houses, tools, weapons, and other daily necessities are made from materials the people collect from the forest.

Most forest peoples grow some food crops, such as plantains, cassavas, yams, and rice. They cut down trees to make small clearings for growing the crops. Then they burn the tree branches and use the ash as fertilizer to help crops grow. After several years, the soil is no longer fertile, so crops do not grow well. The people move on and make a new forest clearing. This farming method is called **shifting cultivation**.

▲ Machiguenga Indians in Peru, South America, have made a clearing in the rain forest for their houses.

● The Mbuti Pygmies are hunter-gatherers who live in the rain forests of Zaire and Uganda in Africa. "Pygmy" comes from an ancient Greek word that refers to a small person. Rain-forest Pygmies are usually under five feet, which allows them to move easily through the forests.

◄ Machiguenga Indians build their homes from materials they gather from the rain forest.

▲ Belaga Penan hunter-gatherers use traditional blowpipes for hunting in the forests of Sarawak, Malaysia, in Southeast Asia.

◀ The Baaka Pygmies are hunter-gatherers who live in the Central African Republic. They hunt animals and collect roots, leaves, fruits, birds' eggs, and honey to eat. This boy is collecting branches to mend the roof of his family's home.

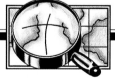

Geography Detective

Many of the houses we live in are made from materials that grow in or come out of the ground. List some of these building materials. Which materials are used to make houses in your area? Where do you think they came from? Do you think any of them came from rain forests?

Rain-forest Settlers

◀ This farmer has cleared part of the Randomafana forest in Madagascar. Rain forests may never regenerate, or grow again, after large areas are burned and cleared by farmers.

▼ Large numbers of trees are cut down to make roads like this one in French Guiana, South America. Roads encourage settlers to move into rain forests. More trees are then destroyed to make way for farmland and settlements.

The population in most rain-forest countries is growing very fast. Many of the people are very poor. Only a few wealthy landowners hold the best farmland, which they use to grow crops or to raise livestock to sell to other countries. Poor farmers are then forced to work less fertile land.

The governments of many rain-forest countries have encouraged the poor farmers to move into

Settlers from Java, Indonesia, are clearing the forest on the nearby island of Sumatra so that they can grow rice on the land.

the forests. When they arrive in the forest, the settlers clear trees using the **slash-and-burn farming** method. Then they plant food crops, such as rice and cassavas. The settlers' crops eventually fail because the soil loses its richness. When this happens, the settlers move on. They clear and burn another area of forest to grow more crops. This cycle of shifting cultivation goes on all the time. In fact, millions of slash-and-burn farmers cut down up to 50 million acres of forestland every year.

In some places, farmers have been encouraged to settle in permanent forest villages, rather than moving from place to place. With help from their governments or other organizations, the settlers can improve the land to grow enough crops to live on.

● Slash-and-burn farming and shifting cultivation destroy more forest than any other use of the land, such as cattle ranching or logging. In 1980 half of the **deforestation** in South and Southeast Asia was the result of this type of clearing and farming.

● Fires that get out of control are a real danger in rain forests. In the early 1980s, one fire alone destroyed more than 15,000 square miles of forest on the island of Borneo.

Geography Detective

Think of three ways that forest fires might start. Why would fire destroy more rain forest after settlers moved there to live? In what ways can burning the trees help shifting cultivators?

Ranches and Plantations

◀ Cattle graze on rain-forest land that has been cleared in Brazil, South America.

Ranchers have cleared huge areas of the rain forest in Central and South America to set up large cattle ranches. Much of the beef from the cattle is exported, or sold, to other countries, where the meat is often made into hamburgers.

Cattle eat grass. But grass does not grow well in poor rain-forest soils after two or three years. When the grass fails, the ranchers move the cattle to new pastures. This means that the ranchers have to clear even more forest to plant grass. For many years, the government in Brazil, South America, gave ranchers grants to pay for clearing the forest for

● Between 1966 and 1978, about 31,000 square miles of rain-forest land were burned in Brazil to make room for 300 huge cattle ranches raising six million cattle.

◀ The Korup rain forest in Cameroon, Africa, is on the left of this picture. The forest has been cleared for an oil palm plantation, on the right of the picture. Oil from the fruits of the oil palm tree is used to make margarine, cooking oils, candles, soaps, and cosmetics.

Sap from rubber trees is called latex. Latex is collected from the trees and sold to companies that make rubber for a wide range of products, such as tires and golf balls. Most of the world's natural latex comes from plantations like this one in Malaysia.

● Rubber trees did not grow in Malaysia until the late 1800s. At that time, the world's rubber came from Brazil. Then the British government asked a botanist to take 70,000 rubber tree seeds from the Amazon rain forest to England. The British grew the seeds and then set up rubber plantations in what is now Malaysia. The rubber industry there was soon bigger than in Brazil.

ranches. The grants were stopped because too much rain-forest land was being destroyed.

Land in rain-forest countries is also cleared for plantations. On these large farms, only one type of commercial crop is grown, such as rubber trees, oil palm trees, or sugarcane. Plantation products are exported and make money for rain-forest countries. But clearing land for plantations also destroys the rain forests.

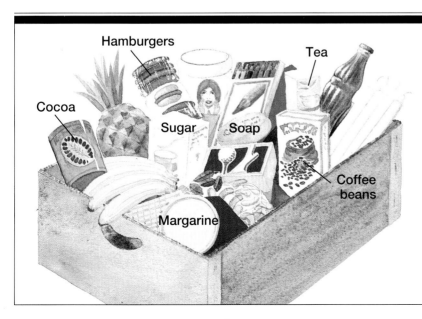

Cocoa, Hamburgers, Sugar, Soap, Tea, Coffee beans, Margarine

Geography Detective

This box contains foods and other products that come from rain-forest plants. Look at the labels on foods you have at home or in a supermarket. Which countries do they come from? Make a list of all the foods you find that come from rain-forest countries.

Logging and Mining

◀ These huge logs are being transported from the Trusmadi forest in Sabah, Malaysia. This forest was once a protected forest reserve.

Rain-forest trees are nearly all **hardwoods**. Hardwood timber, such as teak and mahogany, is used to make buildings, boats, furniture, and many other things. Rain-forest countries, especially Indonesia, Malaysia, and the Philippines, make money from selling this timber to other countries.

To get to the best hardwood trees, loggers make roads, tracks, and large clearings in rain forests. This **clear-cutting** method has been used for years in Southeast Asia, where huge areas of rain forest have been destroyed.

● The Malaysian government is trying out new methods of logging that destroy as little of the rain forest as possible. Helilogging is one method, but it is very expensive. Single trees are felled, then lifted out of the forest by helicopter.

● Nearly all the rain forest in Sarawak, Malaysia, has been destroyed. Unless some action is taken soon, none of the forest will remain.

◀ This logger fells rain-forest trees in Acre, Brazil.

◀ This tin ore mine is in Rondônia, Brazil.

● Large-scale logging has left some rain-forest countries with very little forest. For example, the forests of Thailand in Southeast Asia suffered so much damage from logging that in 1989 the government completely banned commercial logging. People continue to log, however, even though it is illegal.

▶ This iron ore strip mine at Carajas in Brazil is one of the largest in the world.

Some rain forests contain valuable minerals such as oil, iron ore, tin, and gold. Mining these minerals has led to damage. In Brazil, for example, millions of trees were cleared to make room for **strip mines**. Gold miners poisoned rivers and fish with the mercury they use to take gold out of river sediments.

Case Study

The Penan people live in the rain forests on the island of Borneo in Southeast Asia. Their land and their **nomadic** way of life have been threatened by the logging industry. Logging companies took over the forestland where the Penan lived and began to cut down the trees. In 1987 the Penan people protested against this. They blocked the roads into a logging camp so that the machinery could not get in and out. This and other protests helped people all over the world to understand how logging can threaten the lives of rain-forest peoples.

Geography Detective

Find out if there are any wooden things in your home that are made from tropical hardwoods. You may have bowls or furniture that are made from tropical woods such as teak or mahogany, for example. Next time you go to a store that sells hardwood products, check to see if the labels tell you where the wood came from.

Why Save Rain Forests?

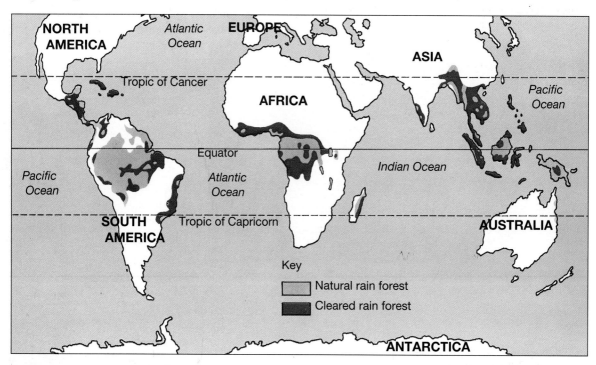

Key

▢ Natural rain forest

▣ Cleared rain forest

▲ Between 1980 and 1990, half of the total area of the world's rain forests was lost. The map above shows how much rain forest remains.

▼ Some scientists think that **global warming** is one of the reasons why ice in the Arctic and Antarctic regions has begun to melt. This has caused the sea level to rise by 4-8 inches.

Carbon dioxide and other gases trap heat from the earth.

Carbon dioxide

Carbon dioxide

Rising temperatures may cause large amounts of snow and ice to melt.

Burning forests and fuels increases the amount of carbon dioxide in the atmosphere.

Melting ice may cause a rise in sea level. Low-lying lands could be flooded.

Forest people lose their lands, their sources of food, and their traditional ways of life.

Burning and clearing rain forests can lead to global warming.

With no trees to protect the soil, rain and wind can wash it away. The soil may block rivers and dams.

Medicinal plants are destroyed.

Rare plants and animals are lost forever.

Bare soil is no longer fertile and can't support crops or trees.

Rainwater easily runs off cleared, bare land and may cause flooding.

▲ This illustration shows some of the results of clearing rain forests.

Saving the world's rain forests is important for many reasons. Many scientists, for example, think that the large-scale burning of rain-forest trees has caused an increase in the amount of carbon dioxide in the earth's atmosphere. Carbon dioxide is a gas that occurs naturally and acts as a blanket around the earth by trapping the sun's heat to warm the planet. But as carbon dioxide and other gases build up in the atmosphere, they trap more heat and raise the earth's temperature. This process is called global warming. Many scientists believe that the earth has warmed up by as much as 1° F since the late 1800s and may get even warmer. Higher temperatures may cause polar ice to melt. Summers might be longer and hotter, and less rain may fall.

● If rain forests continue to be cut down at the present rate, between 20 and 75 species of forest wildlife could be lost each day.

Geography Detective

Write a letter to a politician in your area to explain your ideas about saving the world's rain forests.

23

Managing Rain Forests

Rich countries, such as the United States and many European countries, buy rain-forest timber and beef. By purchasing these products, wealthy countries encourage logging and cattle ranching in rain forests. But rich countries also want to save rain forests and the peoples who live there from more destruction.

The poorer rain-forest countries sell their products and resources to make money. But they want to stop their forests from disappearing, too. How can these problems be solved? Rain-forest countries are looking for ways to use forests without destroying forest ecosystems or harming forest peoples. This method of managing forests is called **sustainable use**.

Friends of the Earth is an international organization that cares about the future of rain forests. It encourages people to stop buying hardwood timber that comes from badly managed rain forests. Changes are already happening. Some stores sell only rain-forest products that come from well-managed forests.

● In 1992 government leaders from all over the world met in Rio de Janeiro, Brazil, to discuss ways to protect the environment, including rain forests. This meeting, called the United Nations 1992 Conference on Environment and Development, is also known as the Earth Summit.

◀ Friends of the Earth made this balloon to draw people's attention to the problem of rain-forest destruction by logging companies.

◀ In 1993 organizations from 25 countries formed the Forest Stewardship Council. The council gives certificates to logging companies that manage forests in a sustainable way. The timber from these forests has a label on it like the one shown here. The label tells buyers that the timber comes from a well-managed forest.

◀ Large areas of rain forest have been saved from destruction by making them into reserves. The man (standing) in the picture is a park warden at Manu National Park in Peru, South America. One of his jobs is to stop people from mining, logging, or ranching in the park.

Geography Detective

Look at the balloon in the photograph on page 24. Can you come up with another way to tell people about rain-forest destruction?

The Way Ahead

Many different projects are taking place to protect rain forests. In Brazil, for example, the government has banned logging and other industries from parts of the forests. In these areas, called **extractive reserves**, forest peoples collect products such as fruits, nuts, and latex. The income earned from selling these types of forest products may be much greater than the income from cattle ranching in the same area.

Workers are planting new types of trees, such as eucalyptus, in cleared areas in Malaysia. These tree plantations cannot replace the original forest habitat. But they do provide timber, help decrease soil **erosion**, and cool the land with their shade.

▲ Some rain-forest countries earn money from tourists who come to visit rain-forest parks and reserves. The tourist in this photograph is hiking on the Choro Trail in Bolivia, South America.

● In 1992 tropical forest peoples formed the International Alliance to protect the interests of forest peoples all over the world. The alliance has written out its goals in a document called a charter. The charter explains what forest peoples want and how they think forests should be managed.

● Some rain-forest animals are dying out because their habitats have been destroyed or are no longer as big in land area. In some places, new trees are planted to make corridors between patches of forest. Animals can use these pathways to move from one patch to another. This gives the animals a much larger area of forest to live in.

◀ Young people from a local school watch birds in the rain forest as part of an environmental education project in Cameroon, Africa.

▶ These villagers are setting up their sawmill in Bainings, Papua New Guinea, to cut a kamarere tree into planks.

Case Study

Village people in the Bainings area of Papua New Guinea, an island country in the South Pacific Ocean, have been given help to buy their own small sawmill. They can move it in and out of the forest very easily. They fell trees one by one, taking each tree from a different part of the forest. In this way, the trees and the soil are not damaged, and the forest ecosystem is not disturbed.

After felling each tree with a chain saw, the villagers use the sawmill to cut the tree trunk into planks. They carry the planks by hand to a nearby store. Some of the wood is exported, and some is sold locally, where it may be used to make buildings or canoes.

▼ Kayapo Indians from the Amazon rain forest in Brazil went to the Earth Summit meeting in 1992 to talk with world leaders about why native forest peoples should have a say in what happens to the world's rain forests.

Geography Detective

Find out about national parks or nature reserves in your state or region. What do they help to preserve? Do you think they are important? Why?

Mapwork

The map on the opposite page shows part of a rain forest in an imaginary country. The town, called Rondo, was built by the government. Poor farmers came to live in Rondo from overcrowded cities outside the forest. The settlers live by growing crops and selling timber. Other people in the town work in the nearby tin mine. The town has a school, a restaurant, and some small stores.

1. Use a ruler and the map scale to work out these distances:
   a) from the tin mine to Rondo, in a straight line;
   b) from the tin mine to Rondo along the roads.
   What is the difference between these two measurements?

2. Use the compass on the map to answer the following questions:
   a) In what direction does the tin mine lie from the marsh?
   b) Is the river flowing from north to south, east to west, or west to east?

3. Make a copy of the map. On your copy of the map:
   a) mark with an A or a B the places where you might find features like the ones shown in photos A and B;
   b) mark with a P a place where a rubber tree plantation could be planted;
   c) mark with an F a place where the river often floods after very heavy rain;
   d) mark with a T a place where heavy trucks and other traffic cross the river.

A

4. Why do you think the settlers who live here may not stay for many years?

B

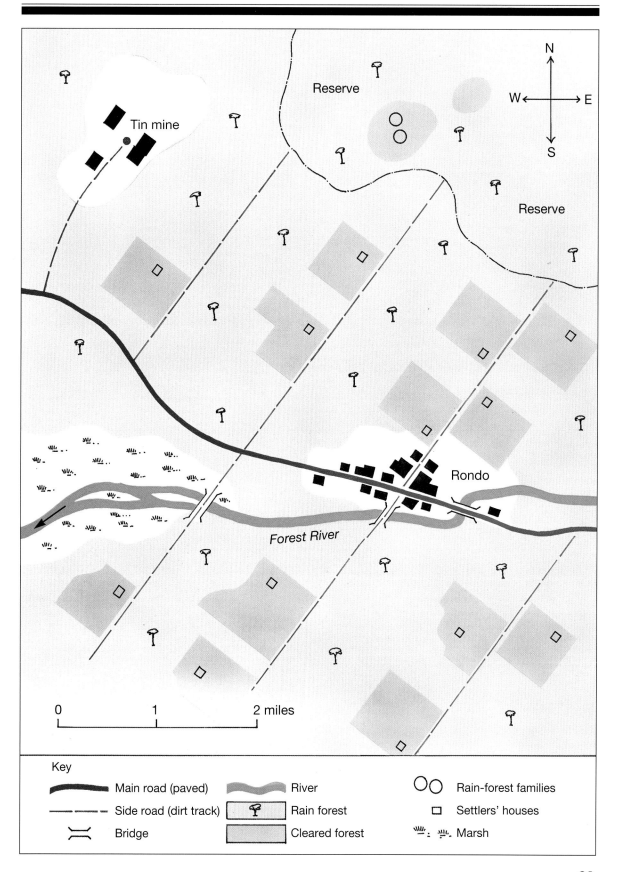

Key

▬▬▬	Main road (paved)	〜〜〜	River	⭘⭘	Rain-forest families
– – –	Side road (dirt track)	🌴	Rain forest	▫	Settlers' houses
⟩⟨	Bridge	▦	Cleared forest	ᬽ᭄	Marsh

29

Glossary

biodiversity: A huge variety of plants, mammals, birds, reptiles, insects, and other living things that are found in a natural environment such as a rain forest.

bromeliad: A tropical plant that usually has upturned, sword-shaped leaves for capturing water. Bromeliads are epiphytes, which receive their nourishment from the air and from rain.

canopy: The high cover of leafy branches formed by the tops of trees in a rain forest.

clear-cutting: Chopping down all the trees in one area.

deforestation: The clearing or removal of forests.

ecosystem: A community of living things and their environment, which work together as a single unit in nature.

endangered species: Plants or animals that are at risk of dying out.

environment: The natural surroundings and conditions, such as soils and climate, that affect how living things survive.

epiphyte: A plant that usually grows on another plant and gets its food and water from the air and from rain.

equator: The imaginary line drawn around the center of the earth on maps and globes.

erosion: The wearing away or washing away of soil or other materials by water or wind.

evaporate: To change water from a liquid to an invisible gas called water vapor.

extractive reserve: A protected piece of land from which workers can harvest products under careful management.

global warming: An increase in average world temperatures. Some scientists believe this is caused by burning forests and fuels such as coal and gasoline.

hardwood: Wood that comes from broad-leaved trees. Tropical hardwoods, such as teak and mahogany, are used for shipbuilding and for making furniture.

hunter-gatherer: A person who fishes, hunts, and gathers food rather than raising crops or livestock.

liana: A climbing plant that winds around tree trunks and branches of rain-forest trees.

nomadic: A way of life in which people move across territory according to the season.

shifting cultivation: A type of farming in which farmers cut down trees to grow crops and then move on to a new clearing when the soil is no longer fertile enough to support crops.

slash-and-burn farming: A way of farming in which farmers clear, burn, and plow the land before planting crops.

strip mine: A mine where minerals are unearthed by stripping off the layers of earth that cover them.

sustainable use: A way of using natural resources, such as rain forests, to produce useful goods continuously without damaging or destroying the resource.

temperate rain forest: A woodland that grows in cool, wet areas such as New Zealand, southeastern Australia, and the Pacific Coast of North America. Many of the trees in these forests are conifers, such as firs and spruces.

tropical rain forest: A woodland of mostly broad-leaved evergreen trees that receives at least 80 inches of rain every year and that is found usually no more than 750 miles north or south of the equator.

tropics: The hot, wet region that forms a wide belt around the earth's equator. The northern border of the tropics is marked by an imaginary map line called the Tropic of Cancer, while the southern boundary is marked by an imaginary line called the Tropic of Capricorn.

wildlife reserve: A protected area where plants and animals are not disturbed by people or industries.

METRIC CONVERSION CHART		
WHEN YOU KNOW	**MULTIPLY BY**	**TO FIND**
inches	25.4	millimeters
inches	2.54	centimeters
feet	0.3048	meters
miles	1.609	kilometers
square miles	2.59	square kilometers
acres	0.4047	hectares
gallons	3.78	liters
degrees Fahrenheit	.56 (after subtracting 32)	degrees Celsius

Index